MONIQUE FELIX

THE COLORS

CREATIVE EDITIONS
MANKATO

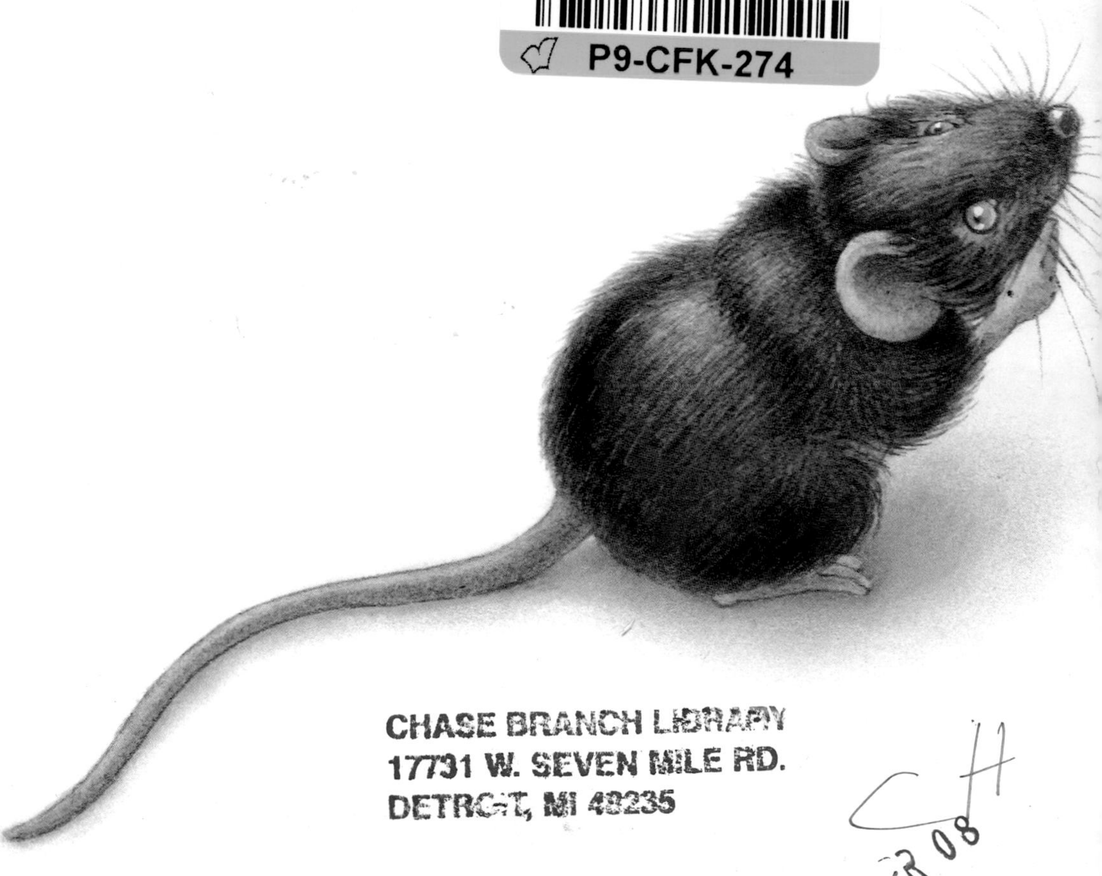

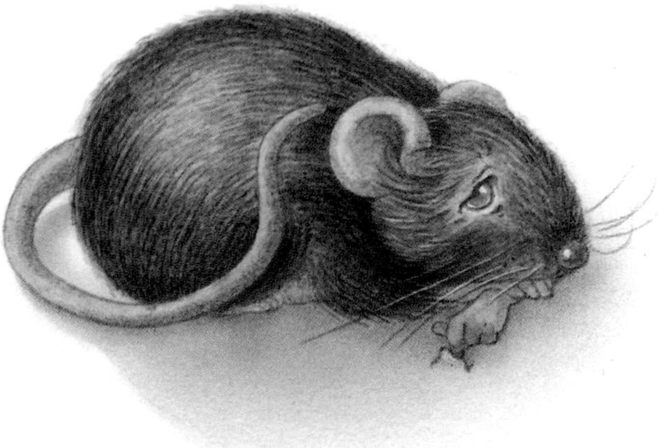

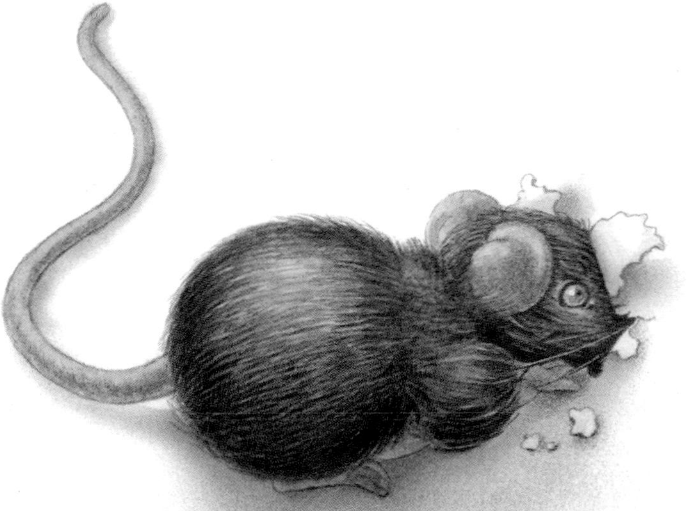

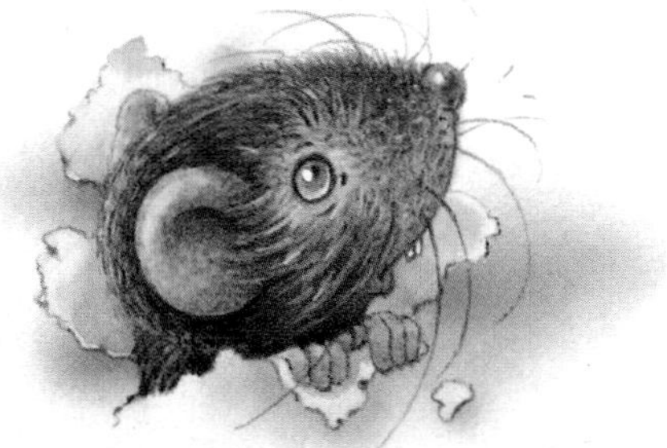

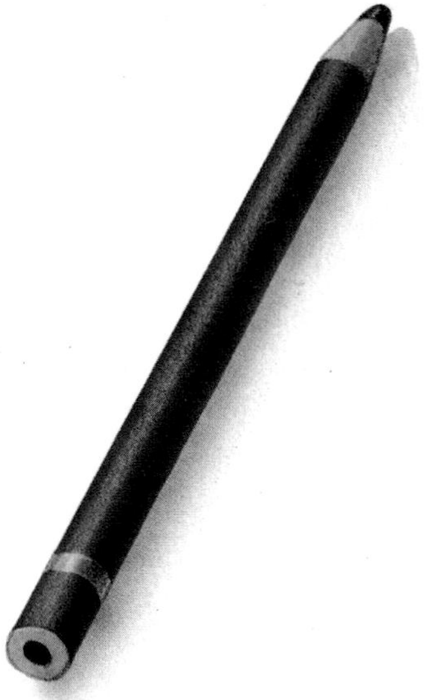

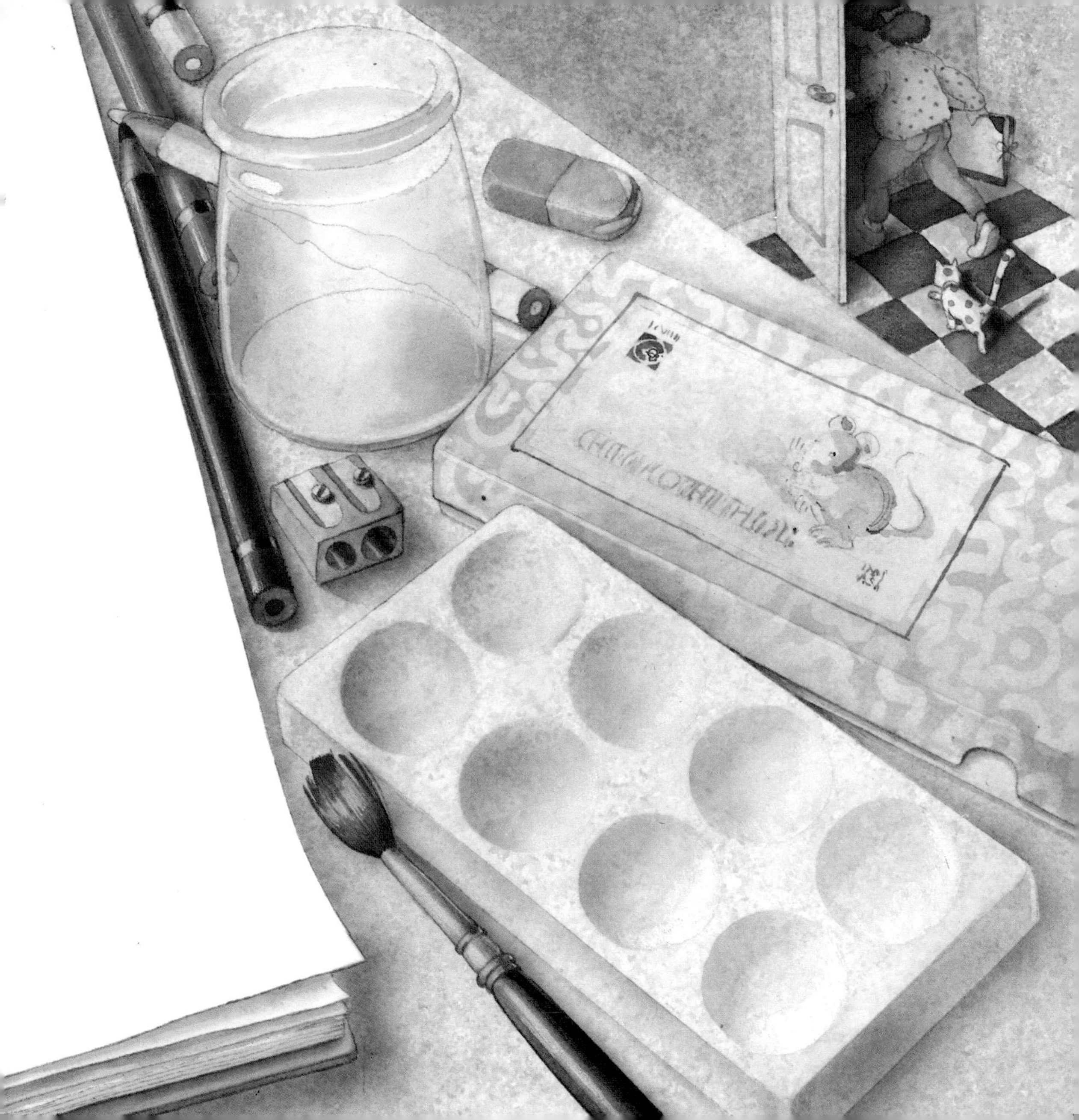

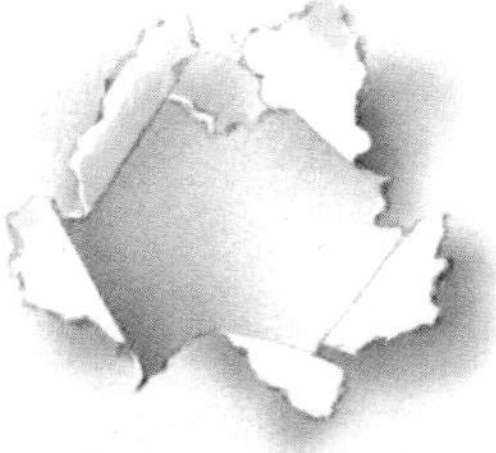

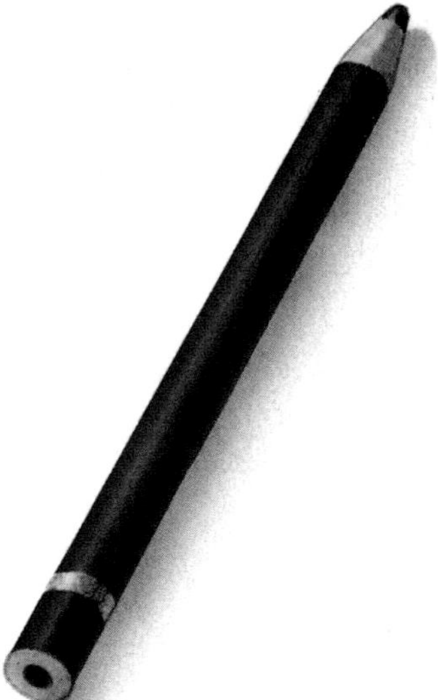

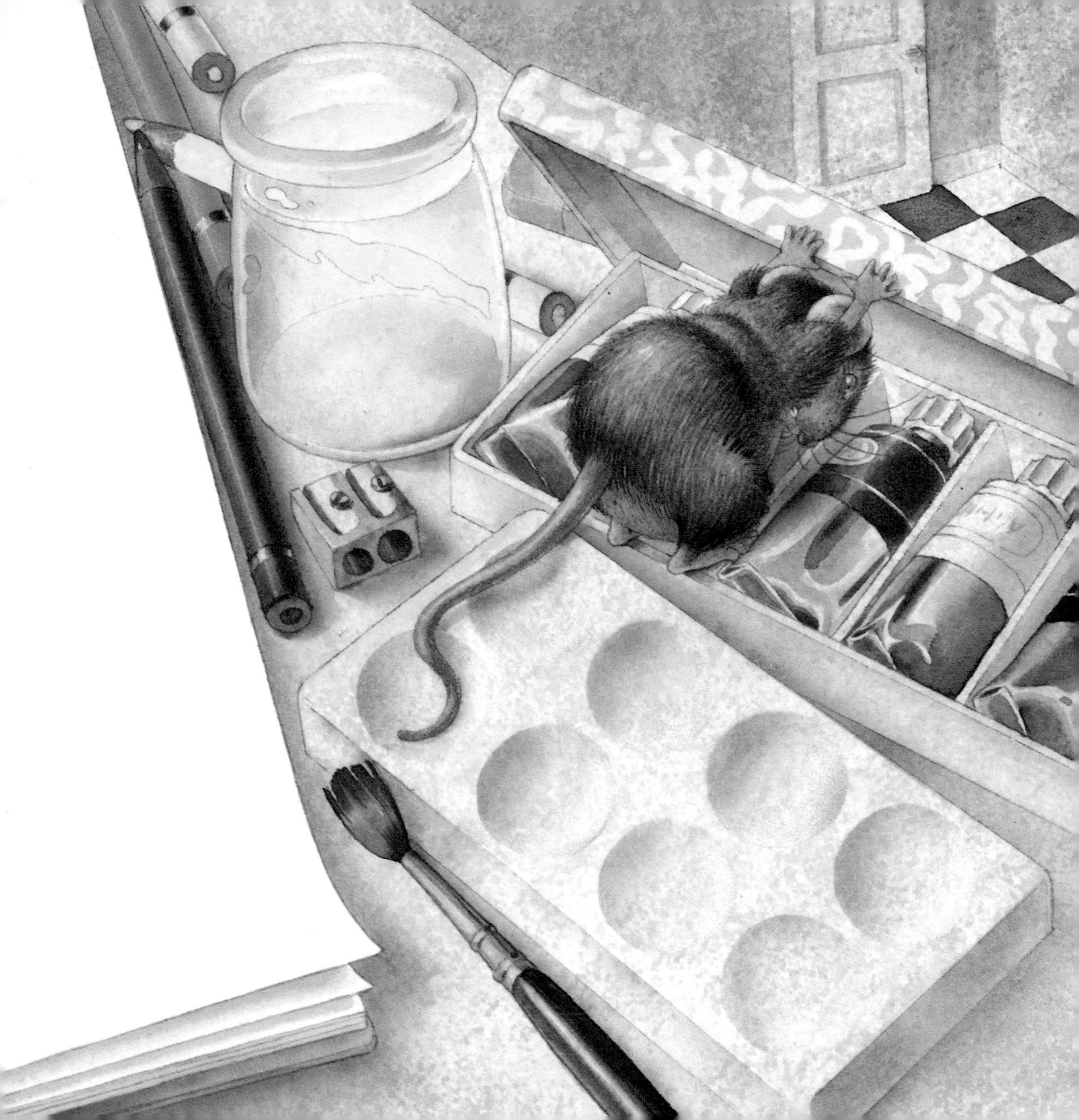

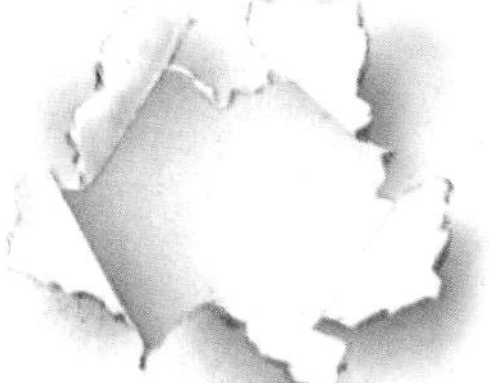

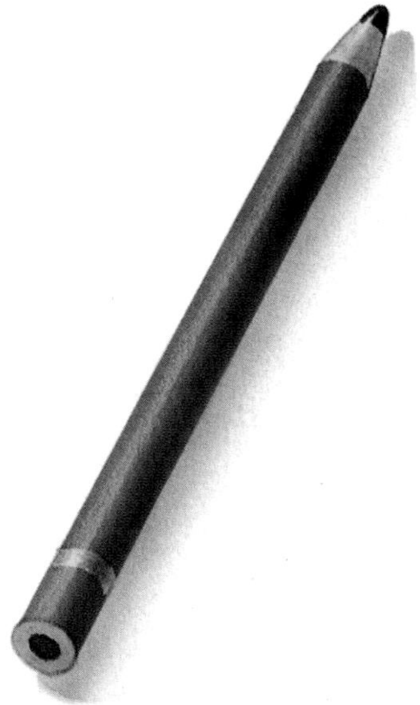

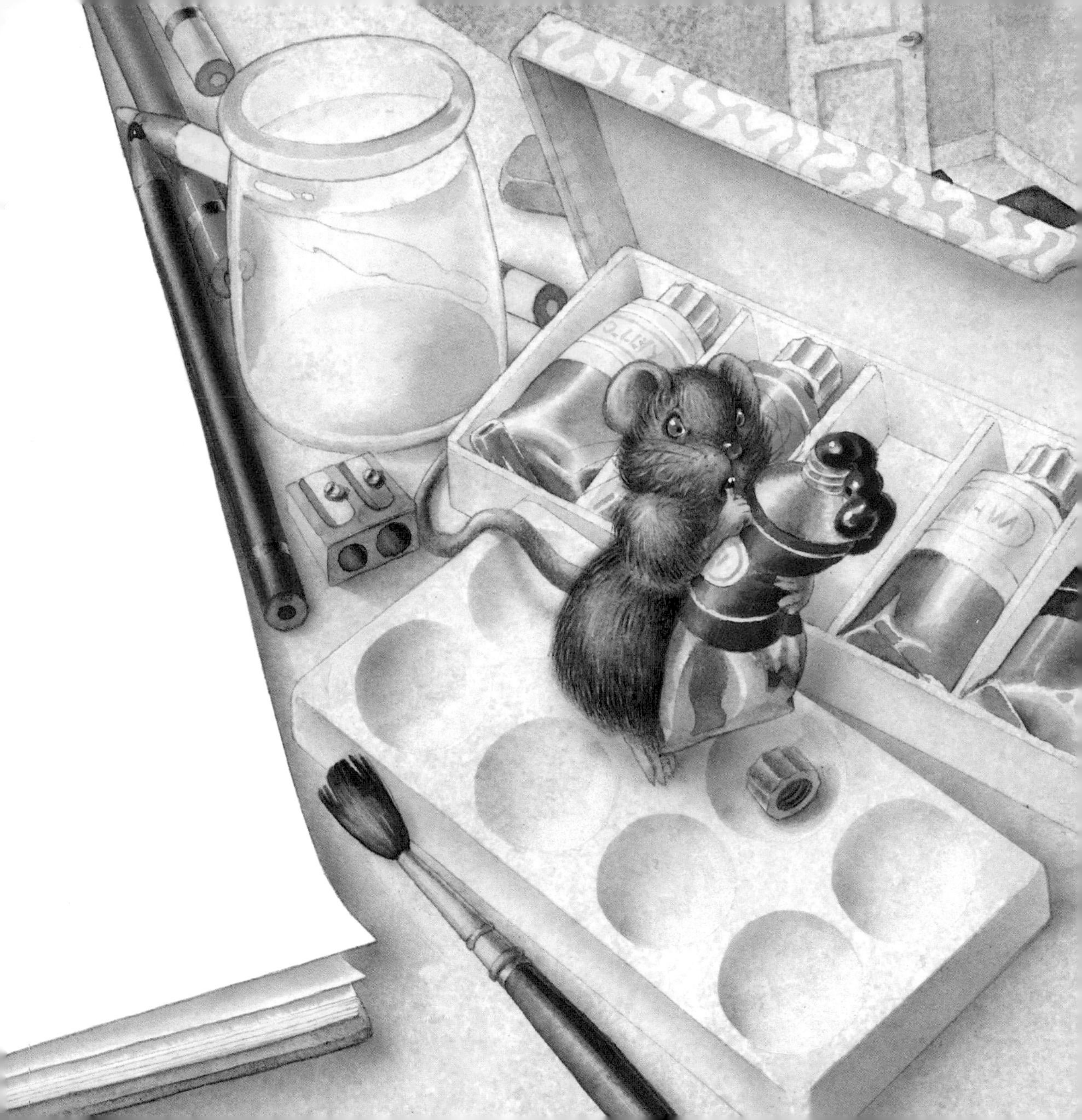

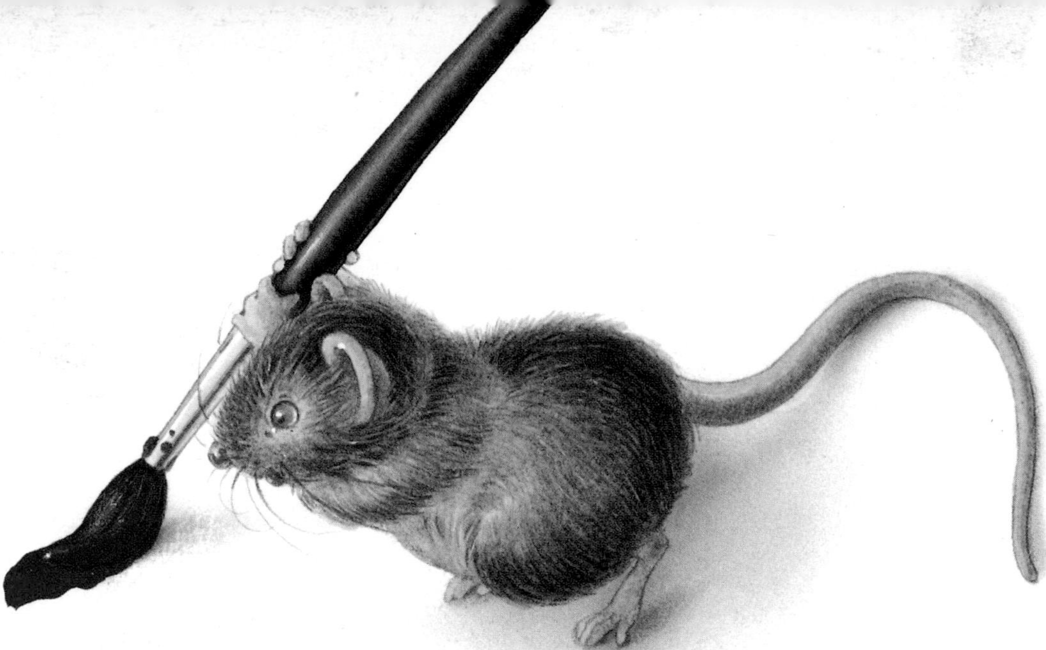

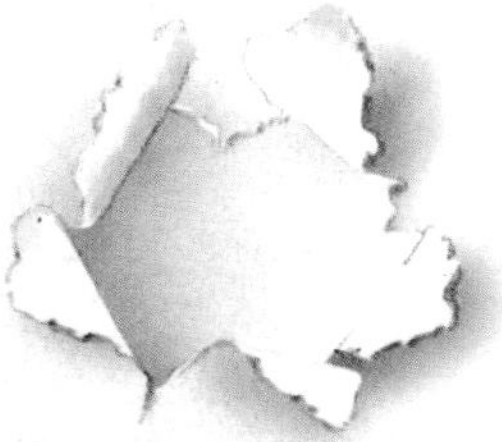

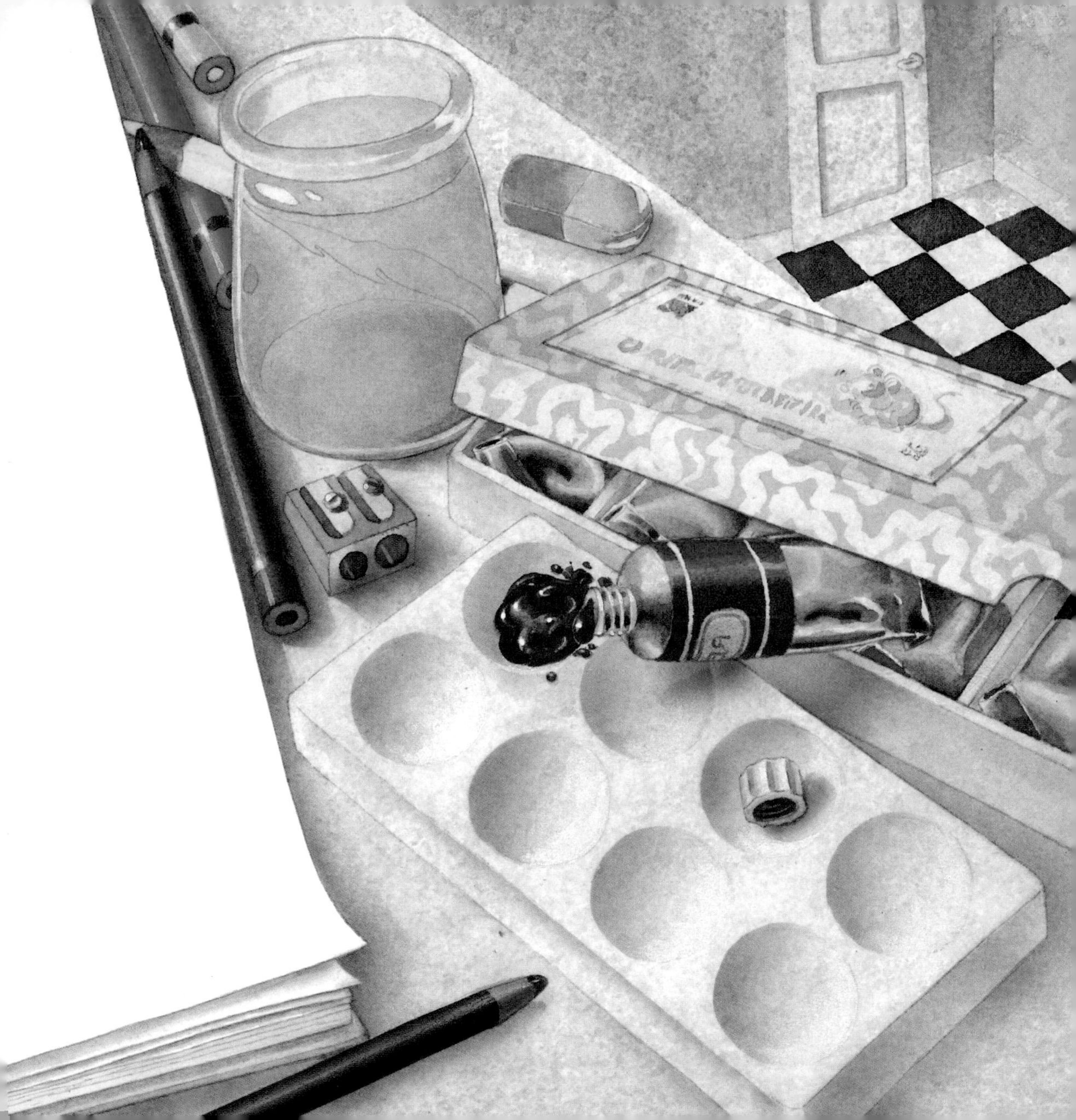

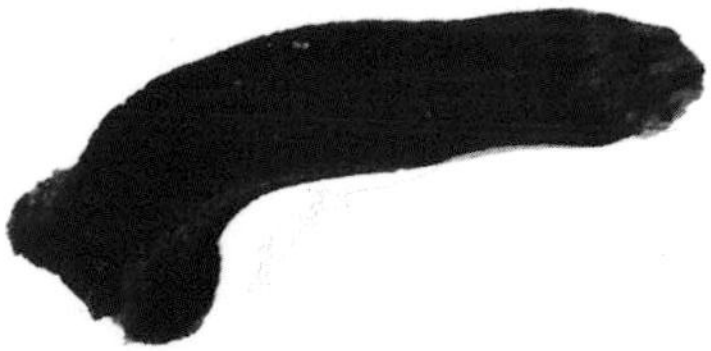

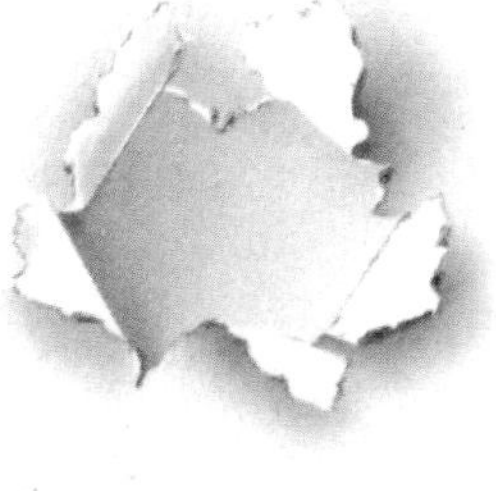

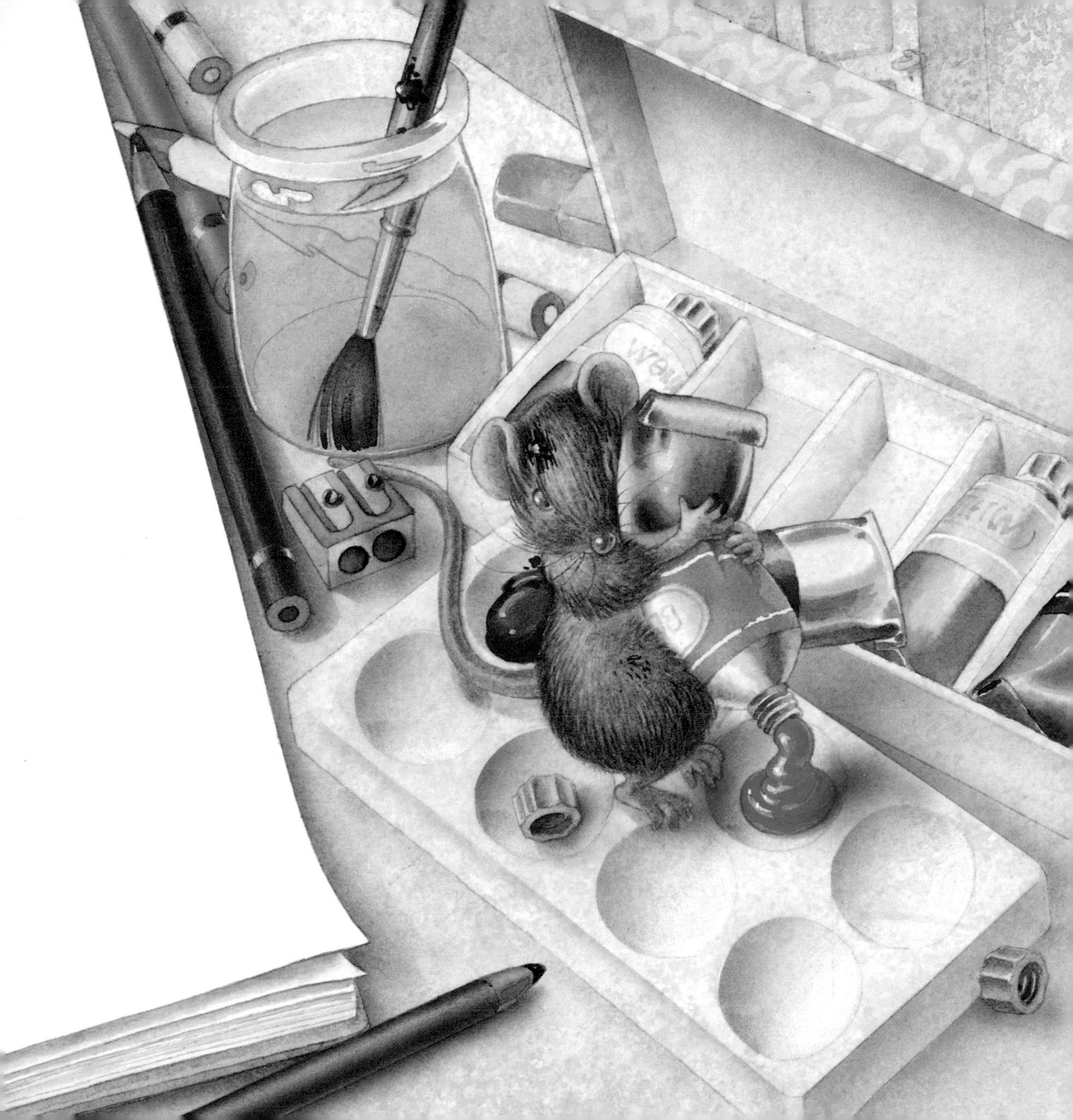

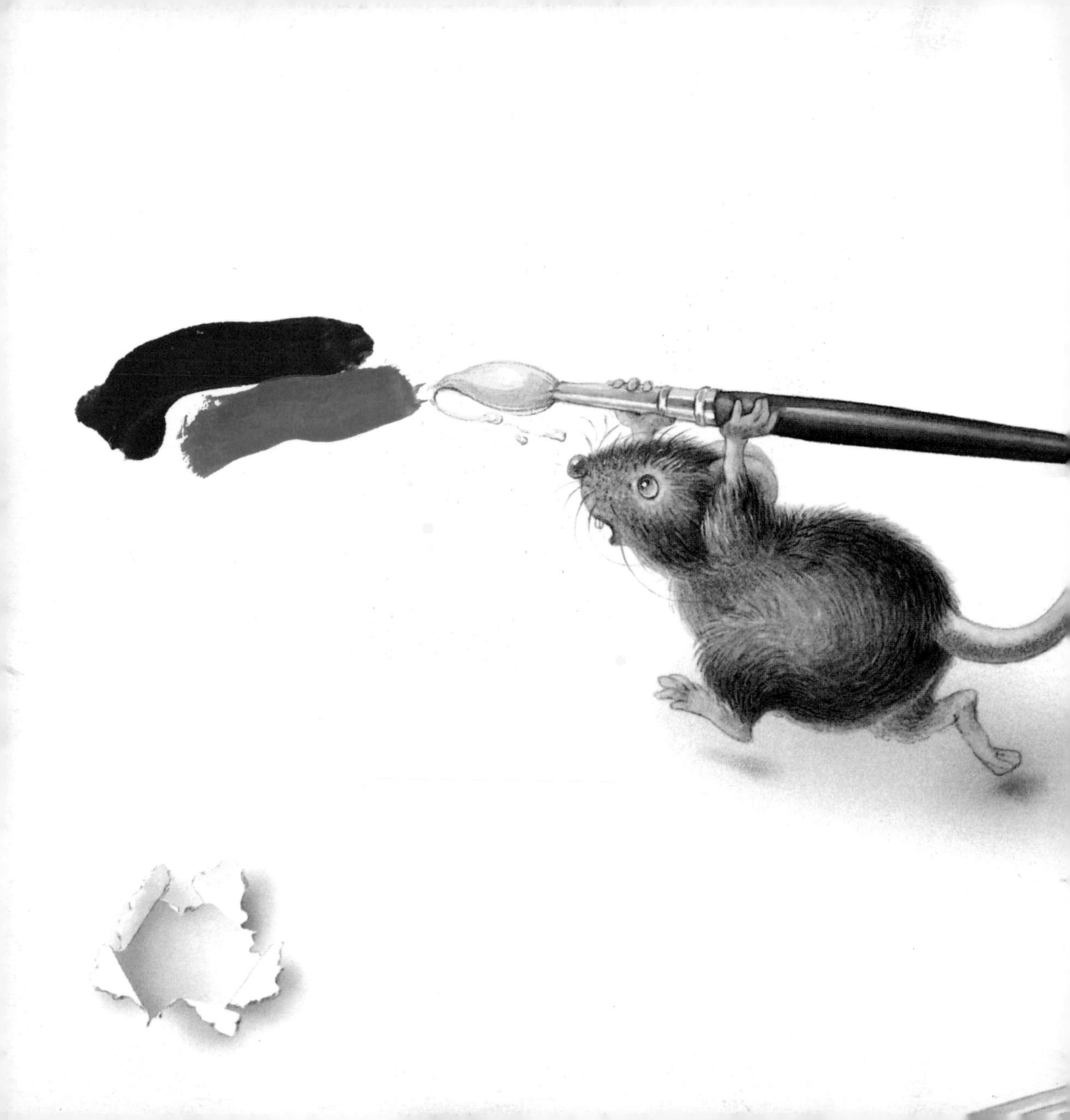

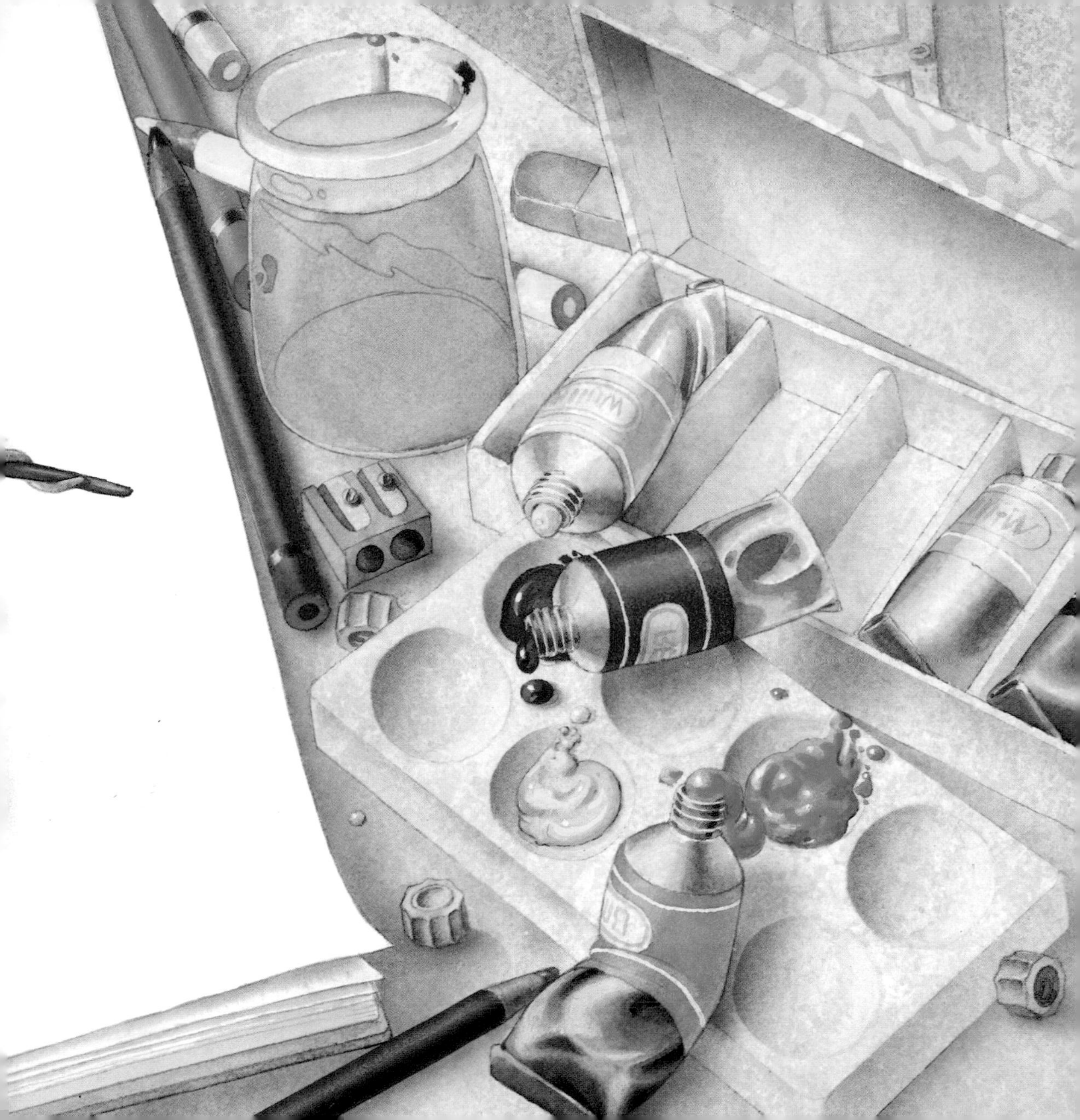

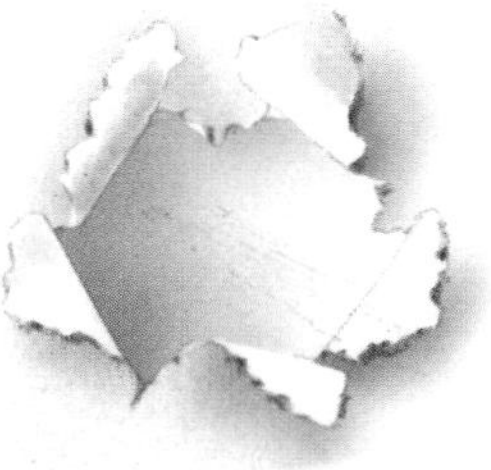

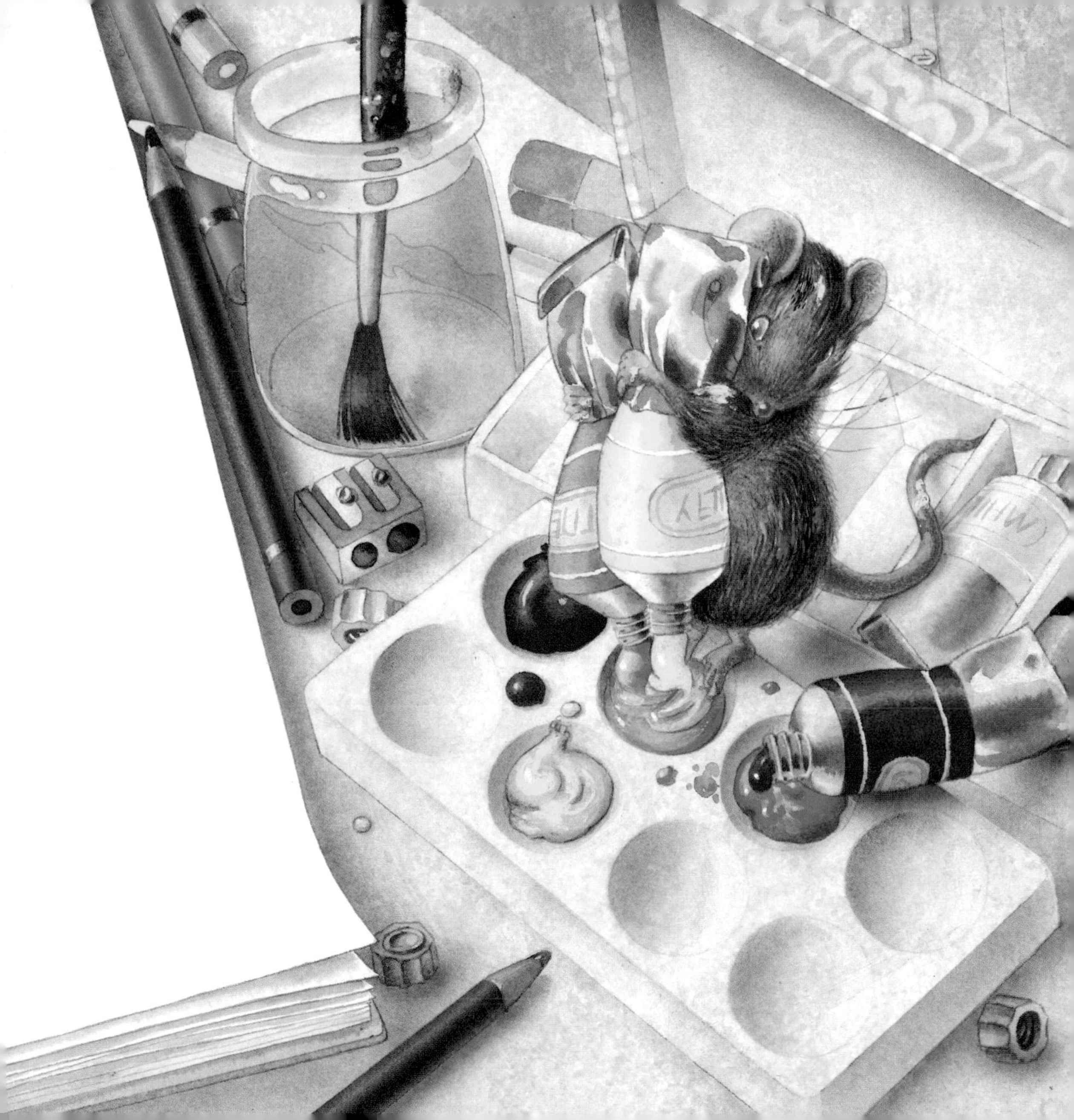

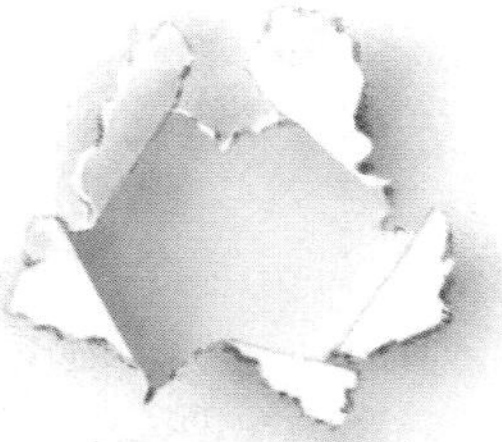

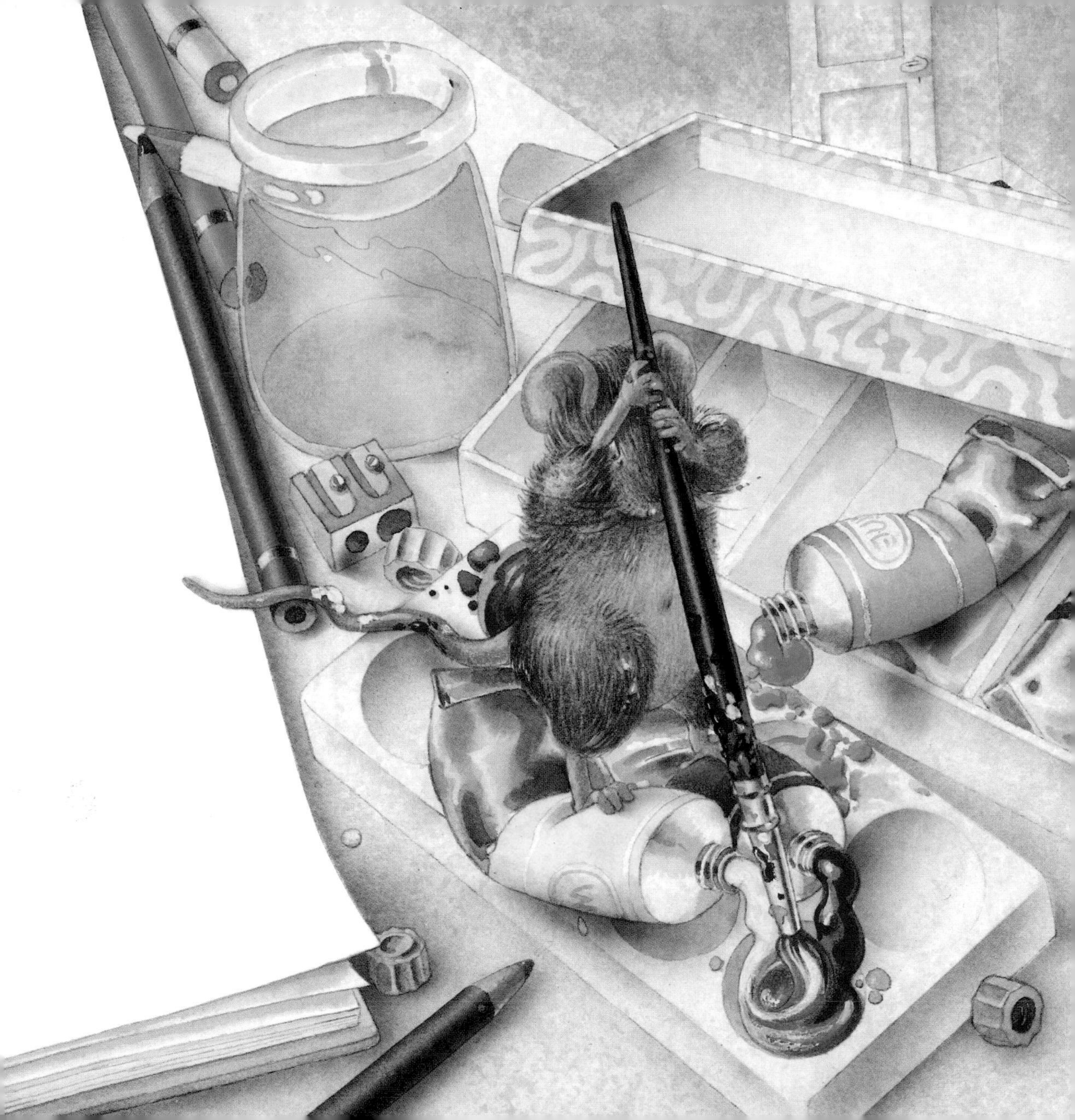

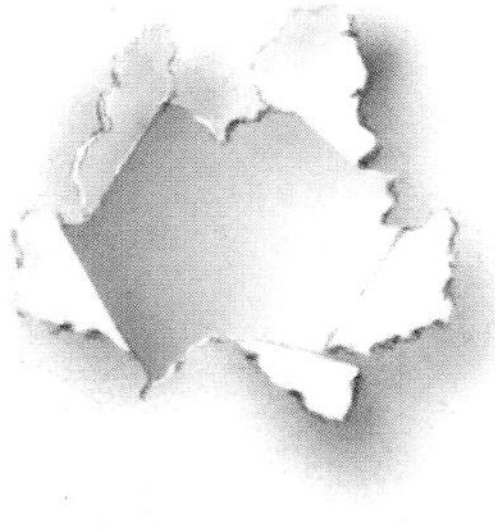

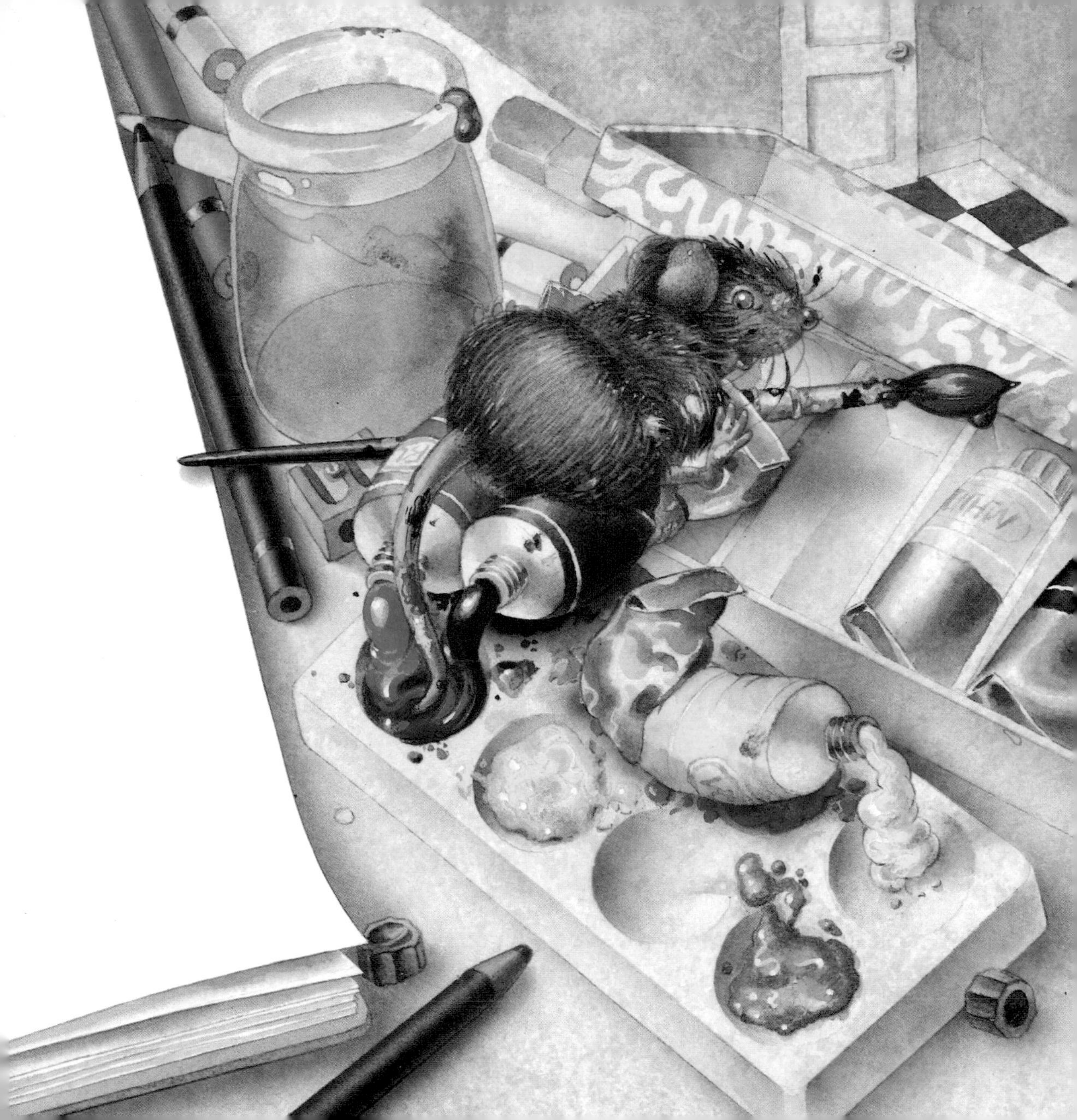

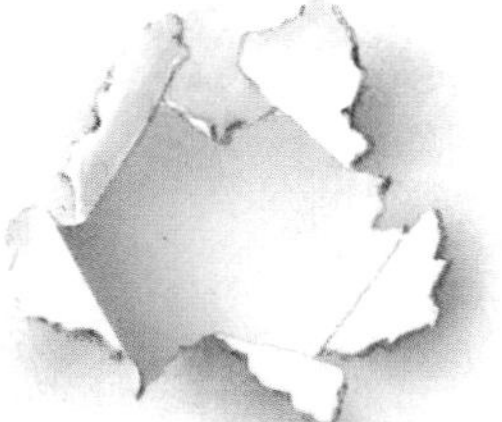

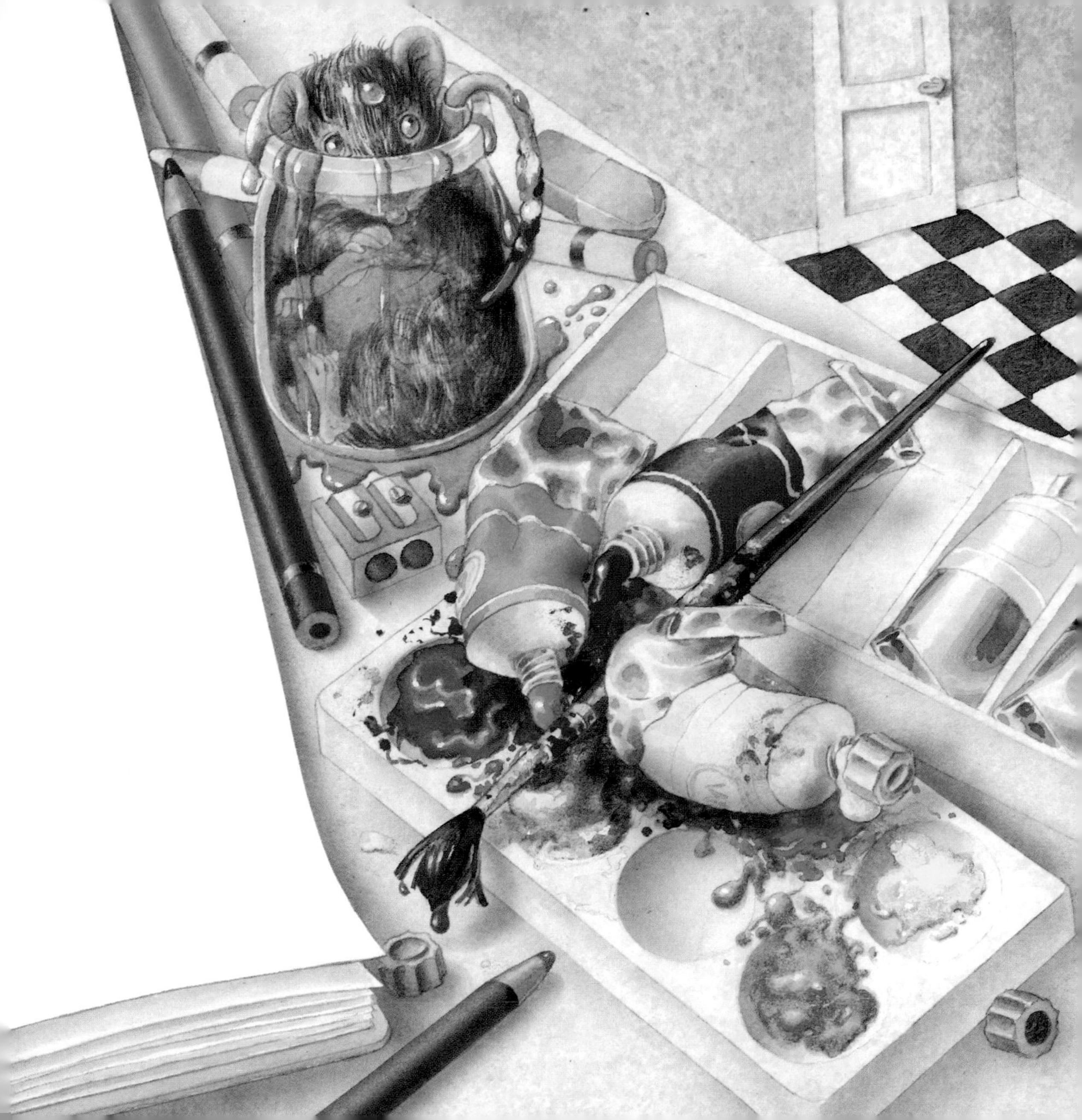

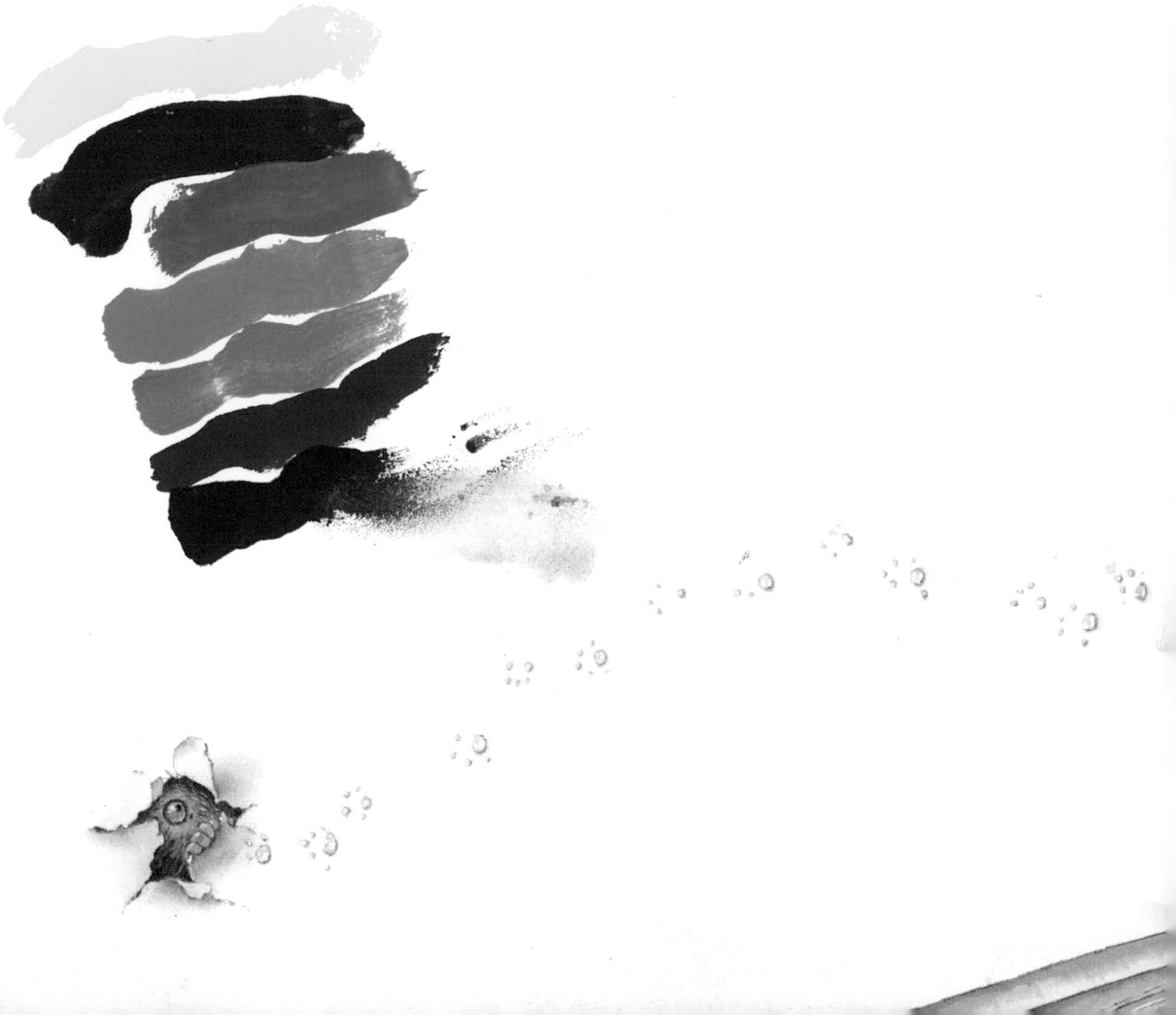

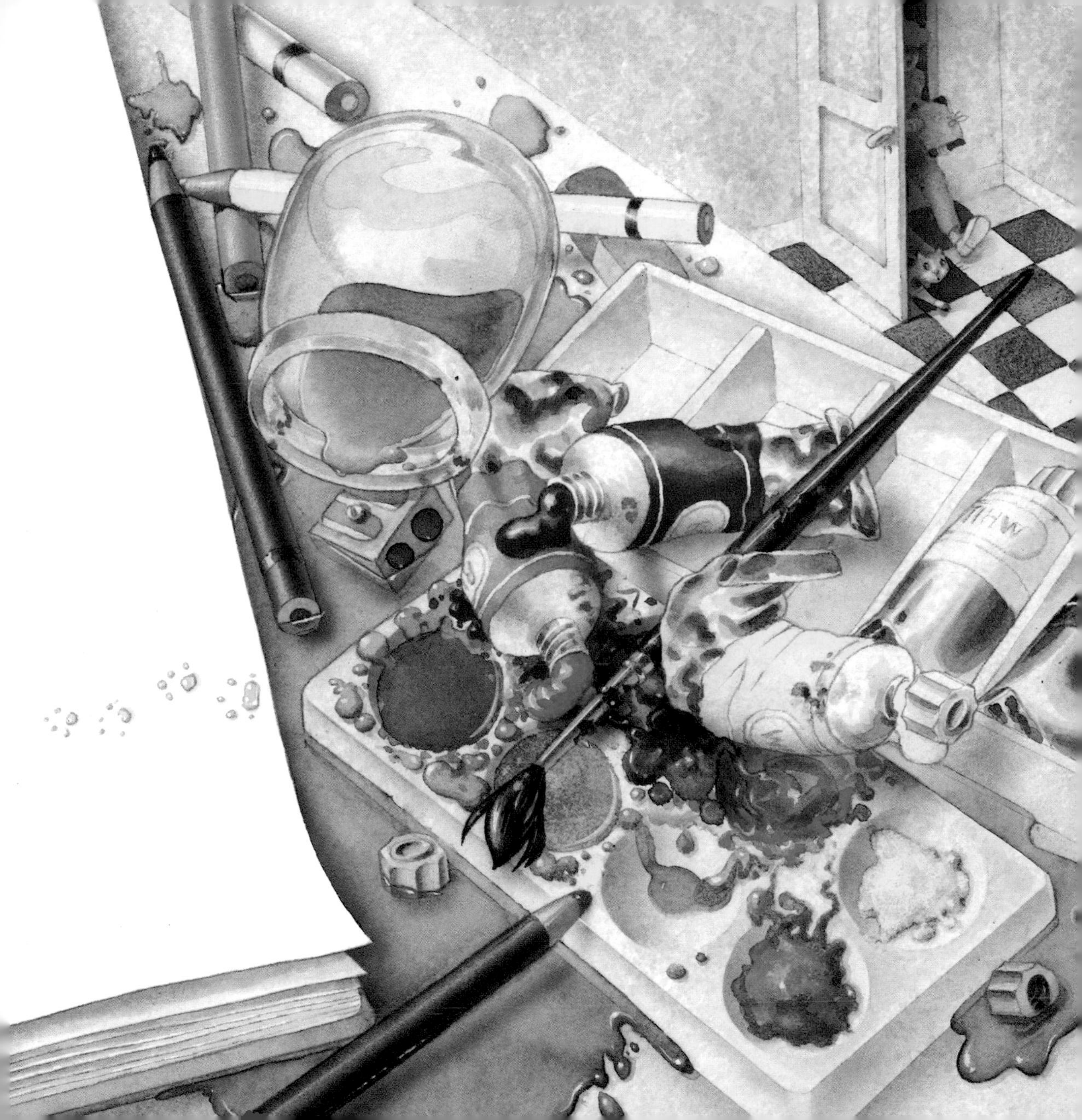

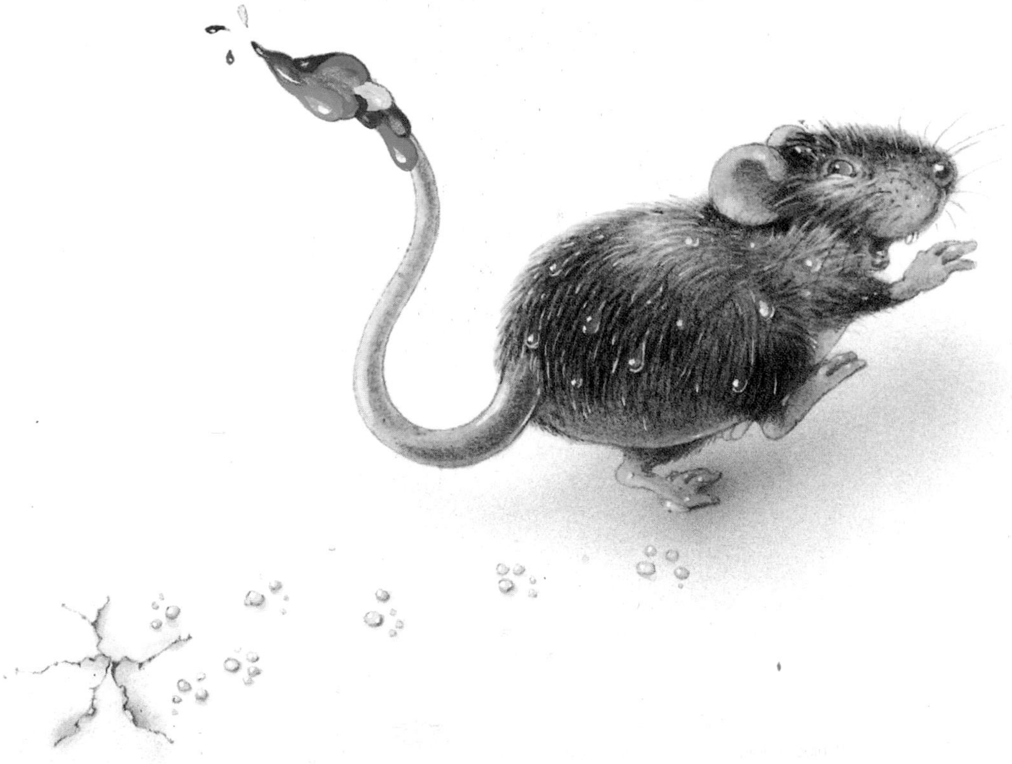